LONGMAN CLASSICS

Da
Copperfield

Charles Dickens

Simplified by D K Swan
and Michael West

Longman

Longman Group UK Limited,
Longman House, Burnt Mill, Harlow,
Essex CM20 2JE, England
and Associated Companies throughout the world.

First published 1987

ISBN 0-582-54160-3

Set in 10/13 point Linotron 202 Versailles
Produced by Longman Group (FE) Limited
Printed in Hong Kong

Acknowledgements

'Photographs © BBC' 1974 for pages 25, 29, 44, 49 56/57 and 69; Dominic Photography for pages 3, 20 and the cover.

The cover background is a wallpaper design called NUAGE, courtesy of Osborne and Little plc.

Stage 4: 1800 word vocabulary

Please look under *New words* at the back of this book for explanations of words outside this stage.

Contents

Introduction

Charles Dickens

Charles Dickens, born in 1812, was the son of a clerk in a government office. His father spent more money than he earned, and Charles Dickens was still a boy when his father, like Mr Micawber in this book, was sent to prison for debt. In those days, men who owed quite small amounts had to stay in prison until the debt was paid.

One result was that Charles's education was interrupted. Another result was that he had experience of the unhappy life of many poor people, including children. In years of hard work in various unpleasant jobs, he met large numbers of people, young and old, rich and poor, happy and unhappy. He had unusual energy and unusual powers of observation. He worked hard to improve his knowledge and at the same time he stored away memories of all the people he met – the men he worked for, the boys he worked with, London scenes and London characters.

He learnt to write shorthand, and he became a newspaper reporter, using his shorthand to record speeches and conversations in different parts of England and finally in Parliament.

He began to write sketches – short stories and descriptions – for weekly and monthly magazines. Readers enjoyed these sketches, especially those which showed Dickens's humour, his rich sense of fun. The *Pickwick Papers* appeared in parts in 1836–37, and the public loved them. Mr Pickwick is the very simple, innocent observer of the behaviour of the people of his time. He is shocked by the wickedness he finds. Sam Weller, his servant, is a worldly-wise, clever fellow who gets Mr Pickwick out of trouble with all the humour of the London "Cockney".

The *Pickwick Papers* were immediately popular, and Dickens was soon in a position to make the writing of novels his one profession. The stories poured from his pen. They all appeared in weekly or monthly parts before being collected in books. Here are the most important of them in the order of writing, with the date of appearance as a book:

1838 *Oliver Twist*; 1839 *Nicholas Nickleby*;
1841 *The Old Curiosity Shop*; 1848 *Dombey and Son*;
1849 *David Copperfield*; 1850 *Hard Times*;
1859 *A Tale of Two Cities*; 1861 *Great Expectations*.

Dickens's characters were much better or much worse than they would be in real life. They were exaggerated in rather the same way as artists exaggerate in their drawings of political and other leaders in newspaper cartoons today. But the readers of Dickens's time accepted such exaggeration. They were perhaps readier to laugh or cry over the novelist's characters and situations than we are today.

The novels of Dickens are full of life, observation and energy, and his own energy seemed endless. His books were popular in the English-speaking countries on both sides of the Atlantic. In later years he travelled widely in Britain and America, reading from his books to eager audiences. His sudden death in 1870 shocked thousands of people who were waiting for his next book. Instead, they bought, and wept over, a picture called "The Empty Chair", showing the desk and chair that he would no longer use.

David Copperfield

David Copperfield is partly autobiographical. That is to say, many of the people and situations Dickens describes come from his own life. But if he knew the people – teachers, lawyers, carriers, fishermen; schools, offices and other places – he used his imagination in describing them. Mr Micawber, for example, is based on Charles Dickens's own father, but Dickens exaggerates. In *David Copperfield,* Mr Micawber is an exaggerated picture of every optimist. The world is full of optimists who expect that everything will be all right *if* ... But none of them is quite like Mr Micawber himself. We would say that he is a personification of optimism.

Dickens's characters often remain in our memories because of a catch-phrase. The one we connect with Mr Micawber is "Something will turn up." Another in this book is "Barkis is willing." Uriah Heep is "very humble", and so on. One does not go far in one's reading of modern English literature without meeting one of these catch-phrases from Dickens or finding a reference to one of the colourful Dickens characters.

Chapter 1
Beginnings

My father died before I was born. One evening soon after his death my mother was sitting by the fire feeling very sad. She looked up and saw Miss Betsy outside the garden fence.

Miss Betsy was my father's aunt. Her real name was Miss Trotwood. Betsy Trotwood lived with one servant in a cottage near the sea. She had always been fond of my father, but she was angry with him when he married my mother.

My mother saw Miss Trotwood at the window, so she hurried to open the door.

"You are Mrs Copperfield, aren't you?"

"Yes. – Please come in," said my mother.

Miss Betsy walked in, and they both sat down. My mother suddenly began to cry.

"Oh! Oh!" said Miss Betsy. "Don't do that!"

But my mother went on crying. Miss Betsy took her face in her hands. "Why!" she cried, "you are only a baby yourself. – Have some tea. What's the name of your girl?"

"I call her Peggotty."

Miss Betsy called Peggotty and made her bring some tea.

"Now," said Miss Trotwood. "Your baby must be a girl. You must name the girl Betsy Trotwood Copperfield. I shall be her friend. Do you know anything about taking care of a house and a baby?"

"Not much," said my mother. "I wish I knew more."

And she started to cry again.

"Don't do that! You will make yourself ill and that will

be bad for the baby."

Peggotty came in. She saw how ill my mother was, and called the doctor.

He arrived and went upstairs to my mother.

Hours passed. Then he came downstairs.

"Well, doctor, how is she?" said Miss Trotwood.

"Mrs Copperfield is quite comfortable," said the doctor.

"I mean the baby. How is she?"

"It's a boy," said the doctor.

My aunt did not say a word. She walked straight out of the house and never came back.

And that is how I , David Copperfield, was born.

The earliest memories that I have are my mother with her pretty hair and youthful shape, and Peggotty with no shape at all and very dark eyes and red cheeks like apples.

My mother and I were both a little afraid of Peggotty.

Peggotty and I were sitting one night by the fire in the sitting room. I had been reading to her. I was very tired – so tired that I could hardly keep my eyes open. I watched her needle passing quickly in and out of the cloth. Then I looked up at her face, which I thought beautiful.

"Peggotty," I said suddenly, "were you ever married?"

"Why! David, what ever made you think of marriage?" she said so quickly that it quite woke me up.

"Were you ever married?" I said. "You are a very beautiful woman, aren't you?"

"Me beautiful? – No, dear!"

There was a short silence.

"Peggotty," I said again, "if you marry a person, and the person dies, then you may marry another person. Isn't that right, Peggotty?"

"You may if you wish to," said Peggotty, "but I don't say

Miss Betsy Trotwood

that you should. People have different opinions."

"What is your opinion, Peggotty?" I said.

Peggotty did not answer.

I read on.

Then the door bell rang. We went to the door to open it. There was my mother looking very pretty, and there was a gentleman with her. I had seen this gentleman before; it was the same gentleman who had walked home with her from church last Sunday. His name was Mr Murdstone.

My mother bent down and kissed me.

"Ah," said the gentleman, "that is a very fortunate young man." He put his hand on my head. I put up my hand and took it away.

"Dear boy!" said the gentleman. "I am not surprised that he loves you!" He bent down and kissed my mother's hand. I was surprised and angry.

"Good night, my dear boy," said the gentleman.

"Good night," I said, but I would not shake hands with him. He turned to go, and, as he did so, he looked at me. He did not look nice. I did not like that gentleman.

We went into the sitting room.

"I hope you have had a nice evening, Mrs Copperfield," said Peggotty, standing up very straight in the middle of the room.

"Thank you," said my mother, "I have had a very nice evening."

"It is pleasant to see a stranger sometimes," said Peggotty.

"Yes," said my mother.

I sat in a chair and fell asleep. When I woke up I found Peggotty and my mother talking, and there were tears in their eyes.

"Mr Copperfield would not have liked such a man," Peggotty was saying.

"Oh!" cried my mother, "you'll make me mad! How dare you speak to me so unkindly! You know that I have no friends to turn to."

"That is a very good reason for speaking. You must not do it! No!" said Peggotty.

"If people like me, what can I do? I can't drive him away. I can't make myself ugly," said my mother. She came to me. "Dear David, she is saying that I don't love you – my own little David."

"I did not say that," cried Peggotty.

"You did! You did! – Am I a bad mother, David? Am I cruel and unkind? I do love you, don't I, David?"

We began to cry together. I went to bed feeling very sad, and I fell asleep still crying.

Next Sunday, the gentleman walked back from church with my mother. He came in to look at our flowers and asked if he might have one. He came again and again. I became used to seeing the gentleman, but I did not like him.

One morning I was with my mother in the front garden when Mr Murdstone came along on a horse. He said that he was going to see some friends who were in a sailing boat at Lowestoft. I was sent upstairs to Peggotty. Peggotty saw my mother and Mr Murdstone walking up and down in the road. She looked very angry. She brushed my hair very hard and hurt me.

Perhaps it was the next day, or perhaps it was a little later when Peggotty asked me to go with her to visit her brother.

My mother was out. Peggotty and I were sitting in front

of the fire. She looked at me several times and opened her mouth as if she were going to speak. Then she shut her mouth without speaking.

"Master Davy," she said at last, "would you like to go along with me and stay for two weeks with my brother at Yarmouth?"

"Is your brother a nice man, Peggotty?" I asked.

"Oh, yes," said Peggotty. "There is the sea at Yarmouth, and boats and ships and fishermen and sand, and there is a boy called Ham for you to play with."

"What will Mother say?" I asked.

"Oh, she will let us go. I'll ask her as soon as she comes home. She's going to stay with Mrs Graper, so we shall not be leaving her alone."

So it was all arranged. The day soon came for our going. We were to go in the carrier's cart.

I remember now how eager I was to leave my happy home.

I remember how my mother stood kissing me at the gate. I cried at the thought of leaving my home. My mother cried too. When the cart began to move my mother ran out of the gate and called to the driver to stop so that she might kiss me once more.

I looked back and saw her standing in the road. I saw Mr Murdstone go up to her. He seemed angry with her for crying because I was going away.

Chapter 2
A visit to Yarmouth

The carrier's horse was the laziest horse in the world. It went slowly along with its head down as if it liked to keep people waiting for their things. We went down many little lanes, leaving a box at one house, a bed at another. Peggotty had a basket of food on her knee. We ate a great deal, and we slept a great deal, but it was such a long journey that I was quite tired, and very glad when we saw Yarmouth.

The country at Yarmouth was quite flat. The sea came in among the houses of the town. It was not easy to tell where the town ended and the sea began.

We came into a street which smelled of fish, and stopped at an inn.

"Here's Ham!" cried Peggotty. "How big he has grown!"

He was a big fellow, very tall, but his face was like a boy's face and he had light curly hair. He was waiting for us outside the inn. He carried me on his back and my box under his arm. Peggotty carried another box. We turned down lanes covered with sand. We passed boat-builders' houses and rope-makers' houses, and all sorts of places where the different parts of a ship are made. At last we came to an open sandy place.

"There is our house, David," said Ham.

I looked in all directions, but could not see any house anywhere. There was a large black boat not far off with an iron pipe fixed in the top of it, and smoke was coming out of the pipe; but I could not see a house anywhere.

"Is that it – that thing that looks like a boat?" I asked.

"Yes, that's it," said Ham.

I was delighted. There was a door cut in the side of the boat and it had little windows in the sides. The top was covered with a roof. What pleased me was that this was a real boat which had been out on the sea. It was never meant to be used as a house on the land. It was such fun to live in a boat on dry land!

We went into the house. It was very clean inside.

There was a table and a clock, and pictures on the wall. There were chairs and boxes used as chairs. Then Peggotty opened a little door and showed me my bedroom. It was a very nice little bedroom in the back part of the boat. The walls were white. There was a looking-glass with shells round it. I noticed the very strong smell of fish in the house. Peggotty said that her brother's work was catching shell-fish.

We had fish for dinner.

Later a dark hairy man came. He kissed Peggotty (who was his sister). He was Mr Peggotty.

"I'm glad to see you, sir," Mr Peggotty said to me. "We are proud to have you here." Then he went off and washed and when he came back his face was very red. I thought that his face was like one of those shell-fish which turn red when you cook them.

We sat by the fire in the evening, and I learned that Ham was not the son of Mr Peggotty but of his brother who was drowned at sea.

When I went to bed I heard the noise of the wind and the sea, and I dreamed that our boat was at sea and that Mr Peggotty was the captain.

The two weeks went by much too quickly, it seemed. I was very sad when the carrier's cart started, and as the cart moved away I felt an emptiness in my heart, but I was glad to be on my way to my mother. I said so. But Peggotty did not seem so happy. She seemed very sad.

We reached the house at last. I remember the cold grey afternoon and the dark rain clouds.

The door opened and I ran towards it full of joy. But there was a strange servant at the door.

"Why! Peggotty!" I said. "Hasn't she come home?"

"Yes, yes, David," said Peggotty. "She's come home. Wait ... I want to tell you something."

"What's the matter?" I asked anxiously. "Why hasn't Mother come to the gate? Is she dead? No! No! She isn't dead?"

"No!" said Peggotty. "I ought to have told you before. You have got a new father."

It was a terrible shock.

"Come and see him," she said.

We went into the sitting room, and she left me there.

On one side of the fire sat my mother, and on the other side sat Mr Murdstone.

Chapter 3
An unhappy time

My bedroom had been changed to another room. I lay on my bed, pulled the sheet over my head, and cried until I fell asleep.

I was awakened by someone saying, "Here he is," and pulling away the sheet. My mother and Peggotty had come to look for me.

"David," said my mother. "What's the matter?"

"Nothing," I said, and turned over.

"You have done this," said my mother, turning to Peggotty. "You have been speaking against me. Oh, David, you bad boy! Peggotty, you bad woman! Oh, what a lot of troubles there are in the world when I've just been married and ought to be so happy."

Then I felt the touch of a hand which was neither hers nor Peggotty's. It was Mr Murdstone.

"What's this?" he said. "Clara, my dear, have you forgotten what I told you? You must be firm."

"I am so sorry, Edward," said my mother. "But it is so hard to be firm."

He whispered in her ear. I knew that he could do with her anything he wished.

"Go downstairs, my dear," he said. "David and I will understand each other."

My mother and Peggotty went out.

"David," said Mr Murdstone, "do you know how I make a horse or a dog obey me?"

"I don't know."

"I beat him – I say to myself, 'I will conquer that animal if I have to beat out every drop of blood in his body.' Do you understand me? – Yes, I see that you understand. Wash your face and come downstairs with me."

"Clara, my dear," he said, when we came into the sitting room, "you will not be made uncomfortable by this child any more."

After dinner a carriage came to the door. Miss Murdstone had arrived. She had brought two black boxes with iron bands on them. She kept her money in a little bag made of iron. She was an iron woman.

She looked at me. "I don't like most boys." She tried to shake hands with me.

"He has no manners," said Miss Murdstone.

We met again next morning at the breakfast table.

"Now, Clara," she said, "I have come to help you. You are far too pretty and thoughtless to do anything that I can do for you. If you will give me your keys, I will take care of all the house matters in future."

My mother began to cry.

"Clara!" said Mr Murdstone. "I am surprised!"

"You talk about firmness," said my mother, "but you would not like so much of it yourself. It is very hard that in my own house—"

"'*My* own house'?" said Mr Murdstone. "Did you say 'my'?"

"I mean *our* house," said my mother, looking very frightened. "It's very hard not to be able to manage anything or do anything in our own house. I'm sure I managed very well before we were married."

"Edward," said Miss Murdstone, "I shall go away tomorrow!"

"Jane Murdstone," said her brother; "be silent!"

"Clara!" he said. "I had hoped, when I married you, to

be able to give you some of that firmness which you need. When my sister, Jane Murdstone, was kind enough to come and help me in this, I expected you to thank her. When you speak as you do, I am pained. My feelings are changed."

"Oh, don't say that!" cried my mother. "I do thank her. Oh, do let us be friends. I can't live where people are unkind to me."

"David," said Mr Murdstone, "this is not a fit scene for a boy. Leave the room!"

I was crying so much that I could hardly find the door. After that Miss Murdstone took complete charge of the house. If my mother said anything or gave any opinion, Miss Murdstone would begin to open her bag as if to give back the keys. Then my mother became frightened and silent.

I had lessons with my mother. My mother was supposed to be teaching me, but Mr Murdstone and his sister were always present, and they used my lessons as a chance for teaching my mother firmness. In the old days, before my mother married Mr Murdstone, I used to enjoy my lessons and I learnt easily. But these solemn lessons with the Murdstones were things of fear and pain. They were a daily trial and sorrow – to my mother as well as to me.

I came into the room and gave the book to my mother, and started to say my lesson. I started speaking quickly while it was fresh in my mind. Then I missed a word. Mr Murdstone looked up, and that frightened me so much that I missed another word. Miss Murdstone looked up: I missed six or seven words. My mother wanted to help me, but she dared not do so.

"Oh, David," she said.

"Now, Clara," said Mr Murdstone, "be firm with the boy. Don't say 'Oh, David.' Does he know his lesson?"

"He does *not* know it," said Miss Murdstone.

"I'm really afraid he does not," said my mother.

"Then give him back the book and *make* him know it," said Miss Murdstone.

"Yes," said my mother. "That is what I meant to do. Now, David, try again. Don't be foolish."

I tried again, and failed at the same place. Mr Murdstone made an impatient movement. Miss Murdstone did the same. My mother tried to help me by moving her lips.

Mr Murdstone came out of his chair. He took the book, hit me on the head and threw me out of the room.

My lessons were like that day after day. Even when I did well I was given more work to do, because the Murdstones did not wish me to sit doing nothing. I became silent, unhappy. My only happiness was a set of books which had belonged to my father. I found them in a room near my own. I had *Robinson Crusoe* and *The Vicar of Wakefield* and a book of travels, and many other books. These books were a way of escaping from the unhappiness of my life.

One morning I went into the sitting room with my book. I saw my mother looking anxious. Miss Murdstone was looking firm, and Mr Murdstone had a stick in his hand.

"I tell you, Clara," said Mr Murdstone, "that I have often been beaten myself."

"Yes, of course," said Miss Murdstone.

"Yes, my dear Jane," said my mother, "but do you think that it did Edward good?"

"Do you think that it did Edward harm?" asked Miss Murdstone.

Mr Murdstone looked at me, still holding the stick in his hand. "Now, David," he said, "you must be more careful than usual." And he held up the stick.

Of course I was worse than usual. I began badly and went on worse. I could not remember anything. At last my mother began to cry.

"Clara!" said Miss Murdstone.

"I am not feeling well today," said my mother.

"Clara," said Mr Murdstone, "you are not yet firm enough to bear the trouble this boy has given you today. David, you and I will go upstairs."

As he led me out of the door, my mother ran towards me. Miss Murdstone said, "Clara! Are you a perfect fool?" I heard my mother crying as we went upstairs.

"Oh, Mr Murdstone, sir," I cried, "please don't beat me. I have tried to learn, but I can't learn when you and Miss Murdstone are near."

He took my head under his arm. I bit his hand. Then he beat me as if he would beat me to death. We made a terrible noise. He was beating; I was crying out; and, above the noise of the beating, I heard them running upstairs, and I heard my mother and Peggotty crying. Then he was gone. The door was locked. And I was lying on the floor.

After a time I became quiet. I listened. There was not a sound in the house. I looked at my face in the glass – so red and swollen that it frightened me. I felt bad – as if I had done some terribly bad thing. What would happen to me? Would I be sent to prison?

Then the door opened. Miss Murdstone came in with some bread and milk. She put them down on the table. Then she looked at me firmly, went out, and locked the door again.

Chapter 4
To school

I woke next morning. I felt quite bright and happy. And then the terrible memory came back to me. I wondered whether I would be hanged, or what would be done to me.

I had to stay there for five days. Those days are like years in my memory. I listened to all the sounds of the house – the ringing of bells, footsteps on the stairs, voices in the street outside.

On the last day I heard my name spoken in a whisper. I went to the door: "Is that you, Peggotty dear?"

"Yes, David. Be very quiet or She will hear us." (*She* meant Miss Murdstone.)

"How is Mother? Is she very angry with me?"

I could hear Peggotty crying. "No. Not very angry," said Peggotty.

"What are they going to do with me, Peggotty dear? Do you know?"

"School. Near London," was Peggotty's answer.

"When, Peggotty?"

"Tomorrow."

Then Peggotty put her mouth close to the keyhole. "David dear," she said, "I have not seen you much lately, but that is not because I don't love you. I love you just as much as ever. But I thought it better not to see you – better for you and for your mother. I thought they would be angry. The day may come when she will be glad to lay her head on Peggotty's arm again. I'll write to you, my dear."

"Thank you, dear Peggotty," I said. "And will you write and tell Mr Peggotty that I'm not so bad as he might think, and that I send my love? Will you please do that?"

She promised.

In the morning Miss Murdstone came and told me that I was going to school. I found my mother at the breakfast table. Her eyes were red with crying.

"Oh, David," she said, "do try to be a good boy."

They had made her believe that I was a bad boy. I tried to eat, but my tears fell on my bread-and-butter.

The carrier's cart came up to the gate. My box was taken down and put on it. Peggotty did not appear.

"Clara!" said Miss Murdstone. "Be firm!"

"Yes, dear Jane," said my mother. "Goodbye, Davy. You are going for your own good. Goodbye, my child. You will come home for the holidays and be a better boy."

There were tears in my mother's eyes.

"Clara!" said Miss Murdstone again.

"Yes, dear Jane," said my mother. "God bless you, David."

Miss Murdstone took me out to the cart. I got in. The lazy horse moved away.

I cried so much that my handkerchief was quite wet. Then the carrier stopped. I wondered why he had stopped. Peggotty climbed into the cart. She kissed me. Then she brought out some paper bags full of cake, which she put into my pockets, and a little bag of money, which she put into my hand. Then she got down from the cart and ran away.

The cart moved on.

After a time I stopped crying. The carrier put my handkerchief on the back of the horse to dry. I looked in the little bag of money. There were three bright coins in it, and a paper: *"For David, with my love."*

I asked the carrier, "Are we going all the way there?"

"All the way *where*?" asked the carrier.

"There," I said.

"Where is 'there'?" asked the carrier.

"London."

"Why, that horse would be dead before he got half that distance. I'm only going to Yarmouth, and the coach will take you to London." This was a long speech for Mr Barkis. (Barkis was the name of the carrier.)

I offered him a cake. He put it in his big mouth and swallowed it whole.

"Did she make that?" he said.

"Do you mean Peggotty, sir? – Yes, she did. She does all the cooking."

Mr Barkis sat looking at the horse's ears, and thinking for a long time.

Then he said, "No husband?"

"No, sir. She is not married."

He sat looking at the horse's ears.

"So she does all the cooking?"

"Yes," I answered.

"Perhaps you will be writing to her?" he said.

"Yes," I answered.

"Well," he said, slowly turning his eyes towards me, "if you are writing to her, say that Barkis is willing."

"'Barkis is willing.' – Is that all the message?" I said. I didn't understand. (Much later I understood that he meant he was willing to marry her.)

"Yes," he said slowly.

"But you will be passing my home tomorrow, Mr Barkis. Could you not give your own message better?"

"'Barkis is willing.' That's the message," he said.

When we reached Yarmouth, the lady in charge of the inn said that dinner had been ordered for me. She led me into a very large room. The waiter brought me my dinner.

"That looks a very big dinner for a little boy," he said. "Shall I help you with it? Let us see who can eat most."

The waiter ate most. He ate nearly all the dinner.

I asked him for some paper and I wrote a letter to Peggotty:

My dear Peggotty,

I have come here safe. Barkis is willing. Give my love to Mother.

Yours with much love,

David

Note. – He says that he specially wants you to know – Barkis is willing.

"Are you going to school?" asked the waiter.

"Yes," I said.

"Where is the school?"

I said, "Near London. That's all I know."

"Oh! I am sorry for that."

"Why?" I asked.

"That's the school where they broke two bones in a boy's side."

This did not make me feel very happy.

The coach came to the door.

The lady of the inn came and looked at me, and led me to the coach.

"Did you eat all that dinner without being helped? – George!" she said to the coach driver, "take care of that child or he will burst."

I got into the coach. It drove away. – At last I reached London in the morning. There one of the masters of the school was waiting for me.

We got into another coach. It drove away and we came

at last to Blackheath.

We walked a short distance and came to a high brick wall. Over a door in this wall there was a board with SALEM HOUSE painted on it.

The door was opened by a man with wooden leg.

"The new boy," said the master.

Salem House was a square, sad-looking brick building. I was led into a schoolroom – the saddest place I have ever seen. It was a long room with three long lines of desks in it. Bits of paper lay on the floor. The walls were covered with ink as if a rain of ink had come through the roof, and there was a strange unpleasant smell in the air.

Mr Creakle, the headmaster, was a fat man.

"So!" he said, "this is the young gentleman who bites. – I have been told by Mr Murdstone that you bite. I know Mr Murdstone. He is a man of strong character. I also am a man of strong character. When I say that I *will* have a thing done, I will have it done."

I was very frightened.

School began next day. One boy – only one – was friendly to me. His name was Traddles, and he became my best friend. I remember the deep roar of many voices in the classroom, and the sudden silence as Mr Creakle came in. Mr Creakle seemed to take a special pleasure in beating boys and he beat poor Traddles most of all.

School went on – and on – and on. Mr Creakle was a bad headmaster who knew very little. The two young masters were bad teachers. Only Traddles made my life there bearable.

At last the term came to an end. I remember travelling in the coach to Yarmouth.

At Yarmouth I climbed into the carrier's cart.

Mr Creakle seemed to take a special pleasure in beating boys

"You look very well, Mr Barkis," I said. – "I gave your message."

"Yes," said Mr Barkis. "But there was no answer. I'm still waiting."

"Have you told her?" I asked.

"No. You must tell her. Say 'Peggotty, Barkis is waiting for an answer.' Then she will say 'An answer to what?' And you must say, 'Barkis is willing.'"

Then he asked, "What is her other name?"

"Clara," I said. "Clara Peggotty."

He wrote these names on the side of the cart.

The carrier put my box down at the garden gate and left me. I walked along the path towards the house, and I went quickly into the sitting room. My mother was sitting with a baby in her arms.

I spoke to her. She stood up and cried out and came half across the room to meet me.

"He's your brother," she said. "David, my dear boy, my poor child." Then she kissed me. And then Peggotty came running in.

Mr and Miss Murdstone were out. So we three had dinner by the fire-side. As we ate, I told Peggotty about Mr Barkis. She laughed.

"What's the matter?" asked my mother.

"Oh, the silly man wants to marry me."

"That would be a good marriage," said my mother.

"No," said Peggotty. "I wouldn't marry him if he was made of gold. – Tell him," she said, looking at me, "that he has never spoken to me, and if he does, I shall slap his face."

Dinner ended. We sat by the fire.

"Peggotty," said my mother, "are you going to be married?"

"Me? No! No! – Never."

"Don't leave me, Peggotty," said my mother. "Stay with me. It will not be for long."

"Me, leave you! Of course not. I shall stay with you till I am an old woman, too old to be of use to anyone."

I told them all about the school.

"I wonder," said Peggotty, "what has happened to David's great-aunt, Miss Betsy Trotwood."

"I suppose she is still in her cottage by the sea. She is not likely to trouble us again."

"Perhaps she might forgive David for being a boy – now that he has got a brother. Do you think David ought to go and see her?"

Then my mother began to cry. "Why do you think David should go away to Miss Trotwood just because I have got a baby brother for him?"

Then they quarrelled, and my mother cried again. And then they forgave each other and my mother said that Peggotty was her "true friend".

The sound of wheels was heard. Mr and Miss Murdstone came in. He gave me his hand – the hand which I had bitten. I could see the red mark on it.

I greeted Miss Murdstone.

"How long are the holidays?" she asked.

"A month," I said.

She wrote down the days on a piece of paper and crossed out one day every morning.

They were very unhappy holidays. The Murdstones did not like me. My mother was afraid to be kind to me when they were in the room, and she was all the time afraid that I might do or say something which would cause trouble. So I kept myself away. I sat in my bedroom and read; or I sat in the kitchen with Peggotty, and when I was with the

Murdstones I remained silent.

Then Mr Murdstone said that I had a sullen character. "I must try to change that character. You keep away from this room and from us as if we had some dangerous illness."

So I remained sadly in the sitting room day after day, and hoped for night to come when I could go to bed and be alone.

The holidays went on. At last Miss Murdstone was able to look up from her paper and say, "This is the last day."

Barkis came to the gate and my boxes were put on the cart. My mother kissed me, and Miss Murdstone said, "Clara! Be firm!" and the cart moved away.

My mother was standing at the gate holding the baby in her arms.

That was the last time I saw my mother alive.

It was about two months after I came back to Salem House. A teacher came into the classroom and told me to go to Mr Creakle.

I found Mr Creakle sitting at his breakfast. Mrs Creakle had an open letter in her hand. She made me sit down and came and sat by my side.

"I have something to tell you, my child," she said. "Your mother is very ill."

I began to cry.

"She is dangerously ill."

I knew what she was going to say next.

"She is dead."

I left Salem House the next afternoon. Mr Barkis was not in the carrier's cart at Yarmouth, but a little fat man with a red face.

Peggotty met me at the gate and led me into the house.

She was crying. She spoke in a whisper, as if she was afraid to wake the dead. I went in. Mr Murdstone was sitting by the fire, weeping. Miss Murdstone was busy writing.

A few days later we all stood together by my mother's grave.

Then, afterwards, Peggotty came into my room and sat down by the side of the bed.

"She has not been well for a long time. She wasn't happy. She sang to her baby, but very softly. She became more and more frightened, so that a hard word was like a blow ... Then one night she said to me: 'Peggotty, dear, I think I am dying. I am very tired. If this is sleep, sit by me while I sleep ... Put your arm under my neck and turn me to you. Your face is far away and I want it to be near.' – And she died like a child that has gone to sleep."

Soon after my mother was put in her grave, Miss Murdstone told Peggotty that she did not need her any more. Peggotty decided to go and stay with her brother in Yarmouth until she was able to find other work.

"Now I've been thinking," she said to me, "that perhaps they don't want you here at present and they might let you come with me."

Miss Murdstone agreed. I was allowed to go with Peggotty.

Mr Barkis came and put our boxes in his cart. He was very polite to Peggotty all the time, but he said little. When we came to the end of our journey he called me to one side.

"You know who is willing? Barkis is willing," he said.

As we walked along the street, Peggotty asked, "David dear, what would you say if I ... got married?"

"To Mr Barkis? I think it would be a good thing,

David at his mother's grave

because you would always have the horse and cart and you could come and see me."

The days passed in Peggotty's house, and gradually my sadness became less.

Mr Barkis came every evening and left a present for Peggotty – fruit, a bird in a cage, a piece of meat, and other strange things. He took Peggotty for walks, and when Peggotty came back, she laughed and seemed glad.

Barkis took Peggotty and me for a ride in the cart. He and Peggotty went into a church leaving me alone in the cart. When they came out he said to me: "What name did I write up in the cart? 'Clara Peggotty.' Well, now it is Clara Barkis."

They had been married in the church.

Soon after this I had to go home. Barkis drove me back in the cart. Peggotty was with him. They left me at the gate. It was a strange thing to see the cart go on, taking Peggotty away.

And now came the darkest part of my life. Mr Murdstone hated me. He and his sister never spoke to me. I lived as a stranger in the house. I would gladly have gone to any school, to the hardest school, rather than live in this way. Peggotty came to see me every week, and I had my story-books. They were my only friends.

Then one day a man named Quinion came to the house.

Mr Murdstone called me into the sitting room.

"This is Mr Quinion of Murdstone and Company. You will work in Mr Quinion's office in London. You will live in lodgings."

Soon I was sitting by Mr Quinion's side in the coach which was taking me to London – a little boy, all alone, going out into the world.

Chapter 5
Mr Micawber

There were three other boys in the office. I did not like them. I was very unhappy. We worked until twelve on the first day. At twelve o'clock, Mr Quinion called me into his room. I went in and found there a small fat man in a brown coat. His name was Mr Micawber.

"This," said Mr Quinion, "is the boy."

"This," said Mr Micawber, with a curious solemn politeness, "is Master Copperfield? I hope that you are well, Master Copperfield."

I said that I was very well and hoped that he was.

"I am," said Micawber, "thank heaven, very well. I have had a letter from Mr Murdstone in which he asks me to receive you in my house in a room which is not being used – at present."

"Your lodgings are at Mr Micawber's house," said Mr Quinion.

"My address," said Mr Micawber, "is Windsor House, City Road; in short, I live there.

"I believe that you may not yet know all the streets of this great city and may have difficulty in discovering the house in which I live; in short, you may lose yourself. So I will come and show you the way this evening."

Mr Micawber put on his hat and marched away. He came back in the evening and led me to his house. There I found Mrs Micawber with four children.

"I never thought, when I was at home with my father and mother," said Mrs Micawber, "that I should ever have to take a lodger. But Mr Micawber has difficulties about money. The people to whom he owes money will not give him enough time to pay."

Poor Mrs Micawber. She was trying to help her husband. There was a notice on the door: "Mrs Micawber's School for Young Ladies", but no young ladies ever came there. The only people who came were people coming for money. They shouted at him in the street and shouted up at the windows. At these times Mr Micawber became very sad and said that he would kill himself, but half an hour later he cleaned his shoes, and went out singing a song, happier than ever. Mrs Micawber was the same: at six o'clock I saw her lying on the floor weeping, but an hour later I never saw her more cheerful, telling me stories about her father and mother and her home. Mr Micawber wept at the beginning of the meal, and sang a happy song at the end of it. He came home in the evening crying out that now nothing was left and he would be sent to prison, yet before he went to bed he was working out what it would cost to put new and larger windows in the house. "Perhaps something will turn up."

They began to sell their things so as to get food.

They dared not carry them out of the house themselves because the men to whom they owed money were watching the place to stop anything being sold. I carried out books and pieces of silver in my pockets or under my coat and brought back the money.

At last the end came. Mr Micawber was taken to prison. I went to visit him there and had dinner with him.

I went back to Mrs Micawber and comforted her. All the furniture was taken away except a few chairs and a table. We lived among these for some days. Then Mrs Micawber went to live in the prison, and I went and lived near, and I used to spend the evening in the prison with the Micawbers. At last the Micawbers were set free. They

Mr Micawber

came and stayed for some time in the house where I was. On their last Sunday, before they went away to Plymouth, I went to dinner with them. At the end of dinner Mr Micawber made a speech.

"My dear young friend," said Mr Micawber, "I am older than you. I have had more experience of life. Until something turns up (which I am expecting) I have nothing to give you except advice. My advice is:

Yearly income £20,

yearly expenses £19, result happiness;

yearly expenses £21, result unhappiness and ruin. The flower is faded, the leaf is dried up, and the sun goes down upon a desert. In short you are ruined, as I am."

In order to make this clear Mr Micawber sang a song and danced.

Next morning they all went away. They had become friends – my only friends. I was miserable at work, and now my only friends had gone – gone to look for something to "turn up" in another part of the country. I decided that I would go to the only relation I had, my aunt, Miss Betsy Trotwood. I packed my box. There was a young man with an empty cart near the corner of the road.

"Will you take this box to the coach?" I said " – the coach which is going to Dover. How much do you want?"

"Sixpence," he said.

I did not like the young man, but I agreed. I put my box on the cart, then took my purse out of my pocket. The young man seized the purse from my hand and drove away quickly. I had no money! I had nothing left in the world! – I started to walk to Dover.

I reached Blackheath and slept in a field near Salem House. Next day I reached Rochester, and from there I walked to Chatham. I decided to sell my coat so as to get food. I went into a little shop with a notice outside: "Best prices offered for old clothes". There was an ugly old man inside the shop.

"Oh, my goodness!" said the ugly old man. "What do you want? Oh, my goodness! What do you want? Grrrrr!"

"I want to know," I said, "if you will buy a coat. Will you give me thirty pence for it?"

"Oh, my goodness!" said the old man. "No! Twenty pence."

"I agree," I said.

But he did not want to give me the money. I waited a long time, and then at last he paid it to me, all in pennies, one penny at a time.

Chapter 6
Dover

I walked on, and at last I came to Dover, and to my aunt's cottage. I was very hungry and tired. My shoes were worn out. My clothes were dirty and torn after the long walk and the nights in fields and woods.

My aunt was in the garden.

As soon as she saw me, she said: "Go away. No boys here!"

"Please, Miss Betsy," I said, "I am David Copperfield. My mother is dead, and I am very unhappy."

I could not say any more. I began to cry.

She went into the house and said to the servant: "Please call Mr Dick."

Mr Dick seemed to be rather mad.

"Mr Dick," said my aunt, "this is David Copperfield."

"Oh, yes, yes!" he said.

"Now don't pretend to be mad, when you are really quite clever," said my aunt. "This is David Copperfield. Tell me, what shall I do with him?"

"Well," said Mr Dick, looking at me, "wash him."

So I was given a bath.

We had dinner. After dinner I told my aunt all that had happened. My aunt listened.

"Well, I can't understand it," said my aunt. "Why do people get married? Your mother got married and then she did it again! And that woman Peggotty, she got married."

She turned to Mr Dick.

"Now, Mr Dick," said my aunt, "what shall I do with him now?"

"Oh," said Mr Dick, "I should put him to bed."

In the morning, I found my aunt sitting at the breakfast table.

"I have written to Mr Murdstone," she said. "And now will you please go upstairs to Mr Dick."

"Yes," I said.

"He is my relation," said Miss Betsy.

"Is he a little mad?"

"His brother was going to put him in a madhouse, but I let him come and live with me. He is a very kind man and gives very good advice, although he is a little mad.

A few days later Mr and Miss Murdstone arrived at the cottage. They sat down.

"You are the Mr Murdstone who married Mrs Copperfield?"

"Yes," said Mr Murdstone.

"And this is her son?" said Miss Trotwood.

"Yes," said Mr Murdstone. "He has run away from his friends and his work. He has caused us a lot of trouble."

"Of all boys in the world, this the worst boy," said Miss Murdstone.

"But," said Mr Murdstone, "I have come to take him back. Is he willing to go? If he is not, my doors are shut against him. And I understand that your doors are open."

"What does the boy think?" said my aunt. "Does he wish to go back?"

"No, no!" I said. "They never liked me. They were unkind to me. They made my mother unhappy. Please, please don't send me back."

"Mr Dick," said my aunt, "what shall I do with this child?"

Mr Dick thought for a long time. Then he said, "I should buy some clothes for him."

Then my aunt looked at Mr Murdstone.

"I will take the boy," she said. "I don't believe a word of what you have said about him. I can see what happened. Before you were married you told his mother that you would be another father to the child, and when you had married her you began to train her. She was a loving woman, but you were cruel to her. You were cruel to her son. You hate him because the sight of him makes you remember how cruel you were."

Mr Murdstone stood by the door. His face was white.

"Goodbye to you, sir," my aunt said. "Goodbye, Miss Murdstone."

They went out. I kissed my aunt and shook hands with Mr Dick.

"I shall call you David Trotwood Copperfield," said my aunt.

My aunt was very kind to me. She shortened my name from Trotwood to Trot.

Mr Dick and I soon became very good friends.

And so I began a new life under a new name, and all that had happened before seemed very far away.

Chapter 7
Canterbury

"Trot," said my aunt one evening, "I must not forget about your schooling. Would you like to go to a school in Canterbury?"

"Yes," I said, "I would like that very much."

"Good," said my aunt. "Would you like to go tomorrow?"

So next day we drove to Canterbury.

"We are going to Mr Wickfield's house first," said my aunt. "He is a lawyer."

We stopped at a very old house whose windows stood out over the road. Two very white stone steps led up to the door, and the windows were made of strange little squares of glass.

When the carriage stopped in front of the door, I saw a white face appear at one of the windows. Then the door was opened by a man called Uriah Heep. He had a white face, red hair cut very short, red-brown eyes, and high shoulders. He was dressed in black. His hand was long and thin.

"Is Mr Wickfield at home, Uriah Heep?" said my aunt.

"Yes, Mr Wickfield is at home," said Uriah. "Please walk in." He pointed with a long hand to the sitting room. There was a picture of a gentleman with grey hair and a beautiful lady with a very peaceful face above the fireplace.

We went into the sitting room. Mr Wickfield, the gentleman in the picture, entered the room. "Well, Miss Trotwood," he said, "what can I do to help you?" He looked some years older than his picture.

"This is David Trotwood Copperfield. I am his great-aunt. I want a school for him where he will be well taught and well treated. Tell me where there is such a school."

"We have a good school here," said Mr Wickfield. "David could not live in the school just at present, but I will tell you what you can do: leave him here. He is a quiet boy, and this is a quiet house. Leave him in my house."

"Thank you very much," said my aunt.

"Come and see my little housekeeper," said Mr Wickfield. We went upstairs into a very pretty room. There was a door in the corner of it. A girl of about my own age came out and kissed Mr Wickfield. She was very like the lady in the picture. There was a peacefulness, a calmness about her which I have never forgotten, which I shall never forget.

"This is my daughter, Agnes," said Mr Wickfield. "Agnes, David Copperfield will stay with us. Will you please show him his room?"

We all went together to see my room. Then my aunt decided to go back to Dover so as to reach it before dark. Mr Wickfield and Agnes went away.

"Trot," my aunt said to me, as she left, "be worthy of yourself. Do honour to me and to Mr Dick. And God be with you. Never be dishonest in anything; never untrue; never be cruel. – Now I must go."

She kissed me hastily, then went out of the room, shutting the door behind her. I thought for a moment that she was angry. But then I looked out into the street, and I saw how sadly she got into her carriage. She had seemed angry only so as to hide her feelings.

In the evening we had dinner – Mr Wickfield and Agnes and I. After dinner, Agnes sang; then she kissed her father good night and went up to her room. I went out and walked about the city looking at the wonderful old houses and the churches. When I came back, I saw Uriah Heep shutting up the office. I felt friendly to everyone, so I went and spoke to him, and when I left, I shook hands with him. How cold his hand was! I rubbed my hand afterwards so as to rub his hand off! When I went to bed his hand was still cold and wet in my mind.

Next morning I went with Mr Wickfield to the school. It was a solemn-looking building in a courtyard. I was introduced to Dr Strong, the headmaster. His clothes were not well brushed nor in good order; his hair was rather long. He looked at me with cold eyes and said that he was glad to see me. Then he shook hands with me.

Sitting at work near him was a very pretty young lady whom he called Annie. I thought that she was his daughter; but when we were going into the schoolroom, he spoke to her as Mrs Strong.

We went to the schoolroom, where about twenty-four boys were busy at their books. They stood up.

"A new boy, young gentlemen," said the Doctor. "His name is Trotwood Copperfield."

A boy called Adams stepped out and welcomed me. He showed me my seat.

I felt strange among these boys, for I had passed through scenes of which they knew nothing, and I knew nothing of their games and their ways. I wondered what they would think if they knew that I had lived with such people as the Micawbers, or if they had seen me walking from London to Dover hungry and in rags.

I was unhappy and afraid of the boys in the school and hurried away as soon as school was finished. But when I came to Mr Wickfield's house, I began to feel all my unhappiness going away. I sat in my beautiful room reading until dinner-time. Then I went down. Agnes was in the sitting room. Soon after that, Mr Wickfield came in.

"You will be happy at Dr Strong's school," he said.

After dinner, Agnes set the glasses on the table, and Mr Wickfield drank. He drank a great deal. Agnes sang. Then she sat by him and talked to him. I brought my books. She looked into them, and she helped me with my work. I seem to see her now with her calm, quiet manner. I seem to hear her calm and peaceful voice as I write these words, and the goodness which she brought to me comes back again. I feel that there is goodness and peace and truth wherever Agnes is . . .

After dinner, Mr Wickfield went to his work. I saw a light in the office and went in. I found Uriah reading a great fat book, following every line with his finger.

"You are working late tonight, Uriah," I said.

"Yes, Master Copperfield. But I am not doing office work. I am learning law."

"I suppose you are a great lawyer," I said, after looking at him for some time.

"Oh, no, Master Copperfield. I am a very humble person. My mother is a very humble person. We live in a humble house. My father's work was very humble work: he was a grave-digger."

"Where is he now?" I asked.

"He is in Heaven," said Uriah. "But we have much to be thankful for. I have to be thankful for living with Mr Wickfield. I hope to become a lawyer."

"Then you will join Mr Wickfield?" I said. "It will be Wickfield and Heep."

"Oh, no, Master Copperfield," said Uriah. "I am much too humble for that. – Your aunt is a sweet lady."

Uriah Heep had a way of moving his body from side to

side when he tried to speak nicely about anyone. It was very ugly. It took my mind away from the nice things he was saying about my friends.

"Your aunt is a sweet lady," he said. "She admires Miss Agnes very much, doesn't she?"

"Oh, yes," I answered, not knowing what to say.

"I hope you do too. I am sure you do," said Uriah Heep.

"Everybody must admire her," I answered.

"Oh, thank you, Master Copperfield, thank you for those words. They are so true."

He seemed to tie his body into a knot and made ready for going home.

"Mother will be expecting me," he said. "If you would come and see us at our humble house, mother would be very pleased."

I said that I would be glad to come.

"Perhaps you will stop here for some time, Master Copperfield? Perhaps you will take over Mr Wickfield's business in the end?" said Uriah Heep.

"No," I said. "I do not think of that at all."

"Oh, yes, I am sure you will. I am sure you will."

He shook hands with me. His hand felt like a fish. I dreamt of it that night.

Dr Strong's school was a very good school. It was very different from Mr Creakle's. The boys were trusted by the masters. We all felt that we had a share in making the school a success. For this reason we all loved the school and wanted to do honour to it.

Some of the boys lived in Dr Strong's house. They told me that the Doctor had been married for about a year to the beautiful young lady whom I had seen. The Doctor was writing a book, but it went on so slowly that it would not be finished within a thousand years. The Doctor was very kind to the poor. There was a story that he gave his coat to a poor woman who sold it to get drink. Then the Doctor saw his coat in a shop and bought it back again – not knowing that it was his own.

I got a letter from Peggotty. She said that Mr and Miss Murdstone had gone away and the house had been shut up. Barkis was a good husband, but very careful with his money. Mr Peggotty and Ham were well.

My aunt came over to see me several times – always at some strange hour. I think she expected to take me by surprise, but she always found me busy, so she gave up these visits. I went to Dover every third or fourth week. Mr Dick came over on Wednesday once every two weeks.

These Wednesdays were the happiest days in Mr Dick's life. He soon became known to every boy in the school. He never played games with the boys, but he watched the games. I have often seen him standing looking at the boys playing on the ice and crying out with joy. The boys loved him. He cut fruit into strange shapes. He made boats and little carts out of all sorts of materials. He had a great respect for "The Doctor" and always stood with his hat off when he spoke to him. He and the Doctor became friends, and the Doctor began to read out from his book to Mr Dick. Mr Dick listened with his face shining with pleasure, but I am sure he did not understand one word of it!

Chapter 8
Uriah Heep

One Thursday evening I met Uriah Heep in the street.

"You promised," he said, "that you would take tea with us. I didn't expect you to keep your promise, Master Copperfield: we are so very humble."

I hadn't decided whether I liked Uriah or hated him. But I said that I would come to tea with him.

"Have you been studying much law lately?" I asked.

"Oh," said Uriah, "my reading can hardly be called study. I have passed an hour or two in the evening sometimes with my law books. I find that rather hard. There are Latin words that I cannot understand."

"Would you like to be taught Latin?" I asked.

"Oh, thank you, Master Copperfield," he answered. "It is very kind of you to make the offer, but I am far too humble to accept it. – Here is my humble home."

We entered a low room. There we found Mrs Heep, who was just like Uriah, only shorter. She received me very humbly.

"This is a day to be remembered, my dear Uriah," she said, "this day on which Master Copperfield pays us a visit. My dear Uriah feared that our humble position prevented you from coming to visit us. We are very humble, we shall always be humble."

"I am sure that you have no need to be so humble," I said.

"Thank you, sir," said Mrs Heep.

I found that Mrs Heep slowly came nearer to me, and Uriah got opposite to me, and they gave me all the best food on the table. They began to talk about their aunts, and I told them about my aunt. They talked about fathers and mothers, and I told them about my father and mother – and then I stopped because my aunt had advised me to be silent on that subject. But I had no chance against Uriah and Mrs Heep. They were too clever with their questions. They got out of me things that I did not wish to tell. When they had learned all they wanted to learn, they began to talk about Mr Wickfield and Agnes – how much business Mr Wickfield did, how we passed the time after dinner, how much wine Mr Wickfield drank – and why, and how sad it was that he drank so much. I found myself telling all sorts of things that I ought not to have told.

I began to wish that I was out of the house. Then I saw a man coming down the street. The door was open. The man looked in at the door.

"Copperfield!" he said. "Is it possible?"

It was Mr Micawber!

"My dear Copperfield, this is a surprising meeting!"

I cannot say that I was glad to see Mr Micawber there.

"I have discovered my friend Copperfield taking a meal with a lady and her son. I shall consider it an honour to be introduced to them."

"We are very humble," said Mrs Heep. "Master Copperfield has been so kind as to take his tea with us. We are thankful to him."

I was very eager to get Mr Micawber away.

"Shall we go and see Mrs Micawber?" I asked.

"I should be very glad," said Mr Micawber.

I went with Mr Micawber to the little inn at which he was staying.

"What are you doing down in this part of the country?" I asked.

"I have relations here," said Mrs Micawber, "and I had hopes that they would be able to get work for Mr Micawber, but they did not seem glad to see us. There was only one thing to do and that was to ask my family to lend me the money with which to return to London. But we came here hoping to do something in the coal trade."

That evening I saw Mr Micawber and Uriah Heep walking past arm-in-arm. I was not pleased. When I went round to the inn next day to dinner, Mr Micawber spoke about Uriah.

"Your friend Heep," he said, "is a man of great understanding."

We had a very nice dinner. Mr Micawber was very merry. He sang songs and we were all very friendly. I do not think I ever saw anyone happier than Mr Micawber was that evening.

At seven o'clock next morning, I received this letter:

> *All is over. There is no hope of any money from Mrs Micawber's relations. I am unable to pay what I owe. I shall soon be in prison. This is the last that you will hear from me.*

I was so surprised and frightened by this sad letter that I ran towards the little inn to see if I could help in any way, but on my way there, I met the London coach with Mr and Mrs Micawber sitting up behind. Mr Micawber was looking quite happy and was laughing at something that Mrs Micawber was saying, and eating sweets out of a paper bag!

My school days came to an end. My aunt and I had often talked together as to what work I should do.

"This is an important matter," said my aunt. "We must

Uriah Heep meets Mr Micawber

not make a mistake. You must try to look at it as a man would, not as a schoolboy."

"I will, Aunt," I said.

"I think that perhaps a little change and travel may be useful to you in helping you to think and decide. You might go down and see the Peggottys."

I went to say goodbye to Agnes and Mr Wickfield.

"I shall feel the need of you very much," I said to Agnes. "Everyone who needs help asks you and is guided by you, Agnes."

"Everyone is very kind to me," said Agnes.

"Whenever I get into trouble, or fall in love, I shall tell you, if you will let me," I said. "Some day I shall really fall in love."

"Oh! But you have always said that your love affairs were real," said Agnes.

"Oh! That was as a child," I said. "My wonder is that *you* have not fallen in love."

Agnes turned away her eyes. Then she looked up to me and said, "There is something I want to ask you. Have you noticed any change in Father?"

I had noticed it.

"Can you tell me what it is?" she said.

"I don't think he does himself any good by drinking so much," I said. "His hand shakes. He doesn't speak clearly, and his eyes look wild. And I have noticed that at those times when he seems to be worst, he is most likely to be wanted for some business."

"By Uriah," said Agnes.

"Yes," I said. "Then he feels that he is not fit for the business, and the next day he is worse, and the next day still worse. A few days ago I saw him with his head on the table, weeping like a child."

Chapter 9
London

My aunt had arranged for me to work in the office of some lawyers, Spenlow and Jorkins, in London, and she paid them money to let me learn the business. So, after a short holiday, I went to London and started work.

I had rooms of my own near their office. It was wonderful to have a new place all of one's own. But sometimes I felt very much alone. That is why I was glad to receive a letter from Agnes, telling me that she was in London. She was visiting some friends of ours, Mr and Mrs Waterbrook.

I went to see her at once.

"You haven't forgotten me, then?" she said. "I hope you will never forget me. You must always tell me whenever you get into trouble, or whenever you fall in love."

Then she asked me if I had seen Uriah. "I believe he's going to become my father's partner," she said.

"What!" I said. "Will that fellow become your father's partner?"

"Yes," said Agnes. "I am afraid that is forced on us. My father is afraid of him. He has some sort of power over my father. Oh, Trotwood, I feel as if I had been my father's enemy, instead of his friend. He has made the circle of his love and duty smaller and smaller, so that his whole mind is given to me. His thoughts have been turned too much on one idea and this has weakened him. I have been the cause of his fall."

A few days later I went to a party at the Waterbrooks'. Uriah was there. He kept close to me all the time. He was close to me when I went away. Agnes had asked me to be nice to him, so I asked him to come up to my rooms.

"Oh, Master Copperfield!" he said. "To see you waiting on me and bringing me coffee is more than I could have expected. But so many things have happened that I have not expected. I hope I may be able to help Mr Wickfield. He has been so unwise. If anyone else had been in my place during the last few years he would have had Mr Wickfield in his power."

He closed his long hand as if he held Mr Wickfield in it. I hated him.

"Miss Agnes was looking very beautiful tonight," said Uriah.

"She looked as she always does, nobler and more beautiful than anyone around her," I answered.

"I have a secret to tell you," said Uriah. "Although I am so humble, I love the ground my Agnes walks on."

I could have killed him as he said these words.

"She loves her father very much, and I hope that she may for his sake be kind to me," said Uriah.

I understood his plan. He meant to use his power over Mr Wickfield to force the old man to give him Agnes as his wife.

"There is no need to hurry," said Uriah. "My Agnes is very young still."

Uriah slept on a chair in my sitting room. I dreamed of Agnes that night. She seemed to be praying me to save her. When I awoke I went into the next room and saw Uriah lying there with his legs out and his mouth open, and I wished I dared kill him.

About a month later, Mr and Mrs Micawber came to supper at my lodgings. I had met Traddles, my old school friend at Salem House, and he joined us. He had worked hard at his law studies, and he had become a very successful lawyer.

The next morning, I received a letter from Yarmouth. Mr Barkis was very ill. I decided to go at once.

I reached Yarmouth. Peggotty took me in her arms and thanked me again and again for being such a comfort to her. Then she asked me to come upstairs.

"Mr Barkis always liked you. He often talked of you. He is asleep now, but if he wakes up he will be glad to see you. It will make him brighter."

It did not seem to me that anything could make Barkis brighter. Time and the world were slipping away from him.

"Barkis, my dear," said Peggotty, "here is Master David. Won't you speak to Master David?"

But he was going out with the tide. We stood there watching him. The sea went out over the sand, and as it went, life slowly passed away from him. He began to talk – something about driving to school. Then he opened his eyes and said to me with a smile, "Barkis is willing."

The sea had gone out. He went out with the tide.

I stayed in Yarmouth for the funeral, but I had to go back to London the next day. I went to say goodbye that night.

Mr Peggotty was smoking by the fire. Peggotty was sitting mending clothes.

"Well, Peggotty," I said, "how are you?"

"She's easy in her mind," said Mr Peggotty. "She did her duty to Barkis, and he has done his duty to her, and it's all right."

"Come to London with me, Peggotty," I said. "The change will be good for you."

David comforts Peggotty

Chapter 10
My aunt is ruined

I came back to my lodgings with Peggotty. When I got there I was surprised to find the door open and I heard voices inside. I went in and found my aunt and Mr Dick! My aunt was sitting on a lot of boxes.

"My dear Aunt!" I cried. "This is an unexpected pleasure. You remember my aunt, Peggotty?"

"Hello," said my aunt to Peggotty. "How are you? Don't call the woman by that odd name, Trot. She has married and got another name. What is your name now?"

"Barkis," said Peggotty.

"Well, that's better. How do you do, Barkis."

We had tea. From time to time I saw my aunt looking at me strangely. I wondered what the reason was.

"Trot," said my aunt at last, when she had finished tea, "Trot, you must be firm and trust your own strength."

"Yes, Aunt."

"Why do you think I am sitting on all these boxes?"

"I don't know," I said.

"Because," said my aunt, "they are all that I have! I am ruined, my dear."

If the house and every one of us in it had fallen into the river, I could not have been more surprised.

"Dick knows it," said my aunt. "I am ruined. All that I have in the world is in this room. Barkis, I want to get a bed for this gentleman tonight. Anything will do."

Then she put her arms round my neck and said that she was sorry only for me. She could not pay for me to continue with Spenlow and Jorkins. In another moment she hid her feelings and said: "We must meet troubles boldly, and not let them frighten us. We must live through our troubles, Trot."

As I came away from telling the lawyers that I must leave, I heard a carriage coming behind me. Then I saw a beautiful face – the face of Agnes.

"Agnes," I cried, "oh, my dear Agnes. What a pleasure it is to see you! Where are you going?"

"I am going to see your aunt," she said. She got out of her carriage and we walked together.

"I am not alone in London," she said. "My father is with me, and Uriah Heep."

"They are not partners?" I said. "Curse him!"

"Yes," said Agnes. "He has such power over my father! There is such a change in the house that you would not know it. Uriah and his mother live with us now. The worst thing about their being in the house is that I can't be as near Father as I wish. Uriah Heep is between us. But I hope that simple love and truth will be stronger in the end."

We found my aunt alone. She told Agnes about her losses.

"What is to be done?" she said at last. "The cottage will give us seventy pounds a year. Dick has a hundred pounds, but he needs that for himself."

"Dr Strong has left his school," said Agnes, "and has come to live in London. He would like to have someone to help him with the book he is writing. Perhaps Trotwood can work for him."

"Dear Agnes," I cried, "you are always my good friend."

So I sat down and wrote a letter to Dr Strong and asked to see him next day at ten o'clock.

Wherever Agnes was, there was always some sign of her sweet presence. When I came back, I found my aunt's birds hanging in the window, my chair had been put near the window just as my aunt's chair had stood. Just as I was looking round at this, I heard a knock on the door.

"I think," said Agnes, "that is Father."

I opened the door. Mr Wickfield and Uriah Heep came in. Mr Wickfield was greatly changed. There was an unhealthy redness in his face. His hand shook. It seemed terrible to me that he should have lost his power; that he should be dependent on that creeping creature Uriah Heep. It was as if a monkey were in charge of a man.

"Well, Wickfield," said my aunt. "I've been telling Agnes how I have been dealing with my money. I have been asking your daughter's advice. I think she is the best person in your business."

"I should be happy," said Uriah Heep, "if Miss Agnes was a partner."

"You are a partner yourself," said my aunt, "and that ought to be enough for you. How are you getting on?"

This was said in a very rough voice.

Mr Heep answered that he was getting on well enough.

"If there is anything that we can do to help, if Mother or I myself or Wickfield can do anything, we shall be really glad," said Uriah.

"Uriah Heep," said Mr Wickfield in a low voice, "is active in the business. I agree with what he says."

"Oh, how wonderful it is to be so trusted!" said Uriah.

"Are you going, Father?" said Agnes. "Will you walk back with Trotwood and me?"

"I have business to do," said Uriah, "so I will leave Mr Wickfield with you."

We sat there talking about our happy days at Canterbury. Mr Wickfield, left with Agnes, soon became more like his old self.

We had dinner together. Agnes sat beside him and poured out his wine. When it was dark he lay down. As Agnes came from him towards the window I could see tears in her eyes.

Poor Agnes – she was so good. She filled my heart with thoughts of good. She strengthened my weakness. Oh, Agnes, sister of my boyhood. If I had known then what I knew long afterwards! – There was a beggar in the street, and as I passed he said, "Blind! Blind! Blind!"

I went along the Highgate Road, full of new life and new purposes. I had decided to offer to work for Dr Strong in the mornings and evenings so as to have more money to help my aunt and Mr Dick.

I found the Doctor's house and saw him walking in the garden. I went in.

"Why, my dear Copperfield," said the Doctor, "I am very pleased to see you. As to your idea of working for me, it is very pleasing; but do you not think you could do something better? Seventy pounds a year is very little."

"It is twice what I have, Dr Strong," I said. "I will come to you mornings and evenings."

The Doctor was very happy at the idea of our working together at his dictionary. His pockets were full of pieces of paper all about his work. We decided to begin at seven o'clock the next morning.

Just about this time I received a letter from Mr Micawber asking me to come to see him at his lodgings in London. "You will be surprised," he wrote, "to hear that something has turned up."

When I arrived I found the two young Micawbers on a bed in the sitting room, and Mr Micawber with a broad smile on his face.

"I am going," said Mr Micawber, "to Canterbury. I have been asked by my friend Uriah Heep to help him in his business. My friend Heep is a man of great powers of mind. He won't pay me very much, but he will free me from my debts."

I was surprised at this news and wondered what it meant.

"I believe," said Mrs Micawber, "that if Micawber gives his mind to the law he may rise very high. He might even become a judge. I am afraid that, by starting so low, he may make it hard for himself to rise. Do you think that Mr Micawber might become a judge?"

"He might," I answered.

Chapter 11
Uriah and Mr Micawber

Some months later I went down to Canterbury and visited Mr Wickfield's house. In the little room where Uriah Heep once worked, I now found Mr Micawber.

"How do you like the law, Mr Micawber?" I asked.

"A man of my powers of imagination finds that the law demands too much dealing with facts."

"Does he pay you well?" I asked.

"He has paid off all my debts – most kindly, most fully."

"I should not have expected him to be free with his money," I said. – "Do you see much of Mr Wickfield?"

"Not much. He is a man who means well, but he is of no further use."

"I think that his partner tries to make him useless," I said.

"My dear Copperfield, I am here as a trusted servant, and there are some matters about which I cannot speak freely."

I saw a change in Mr Micawber. There was something between him and me, something which made it difficult for us to be as friendly as we had been in the past.

I found Agnes sitting in her room.

"Oh, Agnes," I said, "I have felt the need of you so much lately. You used to think for me. I came naturally to you for advice and support. When I am with you there is something which changes me so much for the better. What is your secret, Agnes? My trust is in you."

That evening we sat at dinner. Mr Wickfield drank to the health of my aunt, and to Mr Dick. Then Uriah stood up.

After dinner at the home of Mr Wickfield

"I will drink," said he, "to the fairest lady in the land."

Mr Wickfield had his empty glass in his hand. He looked up at his wife's picture. Then he put his hand to his head.

"I am too humble to drink to her health, but I admire her. I love her," said Uriah.

Mr Wickfield's hands were pressed together in his pain.

"To be the father of Agnes Wickfield is a proud thing, but to be her husband ..." continued Uriah.

May I never again hear such a cry as that which her father gave.

"What is the matter?" said Uriah. "Are you mad?"

I put my arms round Mr Wickfield, begging him to be calm. He was mad for the moment. At last he became calm.

"Look at him!" he cried, pointing to Uriah. "Because of him I have given up step by step my good name, my peace and quiet, my house and home."

"Don't be foolish, Mr Wickfield," said Uriah. "There's no harm done."

"I thought that I could trust him because it was in his interest to be true to me, but see what he is!"

"You had better stop him, Copperfield," said Uriah. "He will say something for which he will be sorry."

"I'll say anything!" cried Mr Wickfield. "Why should I not say what I like?"

"Be careful, I tell you!" said Uriah to me. "If you don't stop him talking, you are not his friend. You and I know what we know, don't we? Can't you see that I am humble? If I've said too much, I am sorry."

"Oh, Trotwood, Trotwood," cried Mr Wickfield, "what have I come down to since I first saw you in this house.

Weakness has ruined me. I have been weak in remembering – in remembering my child's mother too much. My natural grief has turned to disease. I have thought it possible to love one creature in the world and not love the rest. Weak in my grief, weak in my love, weak in my escape from the darker side of both. Oh, see the ruin that I am, and I hate myself!"

He fell into a chair and wept.

It was dark when I got into a coach at the inn door. Uriah came to the side of the coach.

"Copperfield," he said in a low voice like a frog's, "I thought you'd be glad to hear that there's no more trouble between us. I've been to his room and we've made everything right. I suppose you have sometimes taken an apple from the tree before it was ready? – But the time will come. I can wait!"

More months passed and then, surprisingly, I received a strange letter from Mr Micawber. "My peace is ended. My power of enjoyment is destroyed. The flower is faded." – And so it went on. I read the letter several times, but could not get its meaning. And yet it seemed to be more important than most of Mr Micawber's letters.

At the same time I received a letter from Mrs Micawber:

> *Mr Micawber is not himself. He is saying that he has sold himself to the Devil. He says that he wishes to be separated from me. He is secret and strange in his manner. I beg you to see him and talk to him.*

I wrote a comforting letter to Mrs Micawber and arranged to meet Mr Micawber at my aunt's house.

We found Mr Micawber in a very unhappy state.

"How is our friend Heep?" I asked.

"If you ask about him as *your* friend, I am sorry. If you ask about him as *my* friend, I laugh! I do not wish to speak about the subject of Heep. – Oh, leave me; leave me to walk the earth as an outcast. Death will settle my business soon enough."

"I hope that Mrs Micawber and your family are well, sir," said my aunt.

"They are as well, madam, as outcasts can ever hope to be," answered Mr Micawber.

"Mr Micawber," I said, "speak out. You are among friends. What is the matter?"

"What is the matter? – Evil is the matter! Wrongdoing is the matter. Thieving and deceiving are the matter! And the cause of all of it is HEEP! – The struggle is over! I will live this life no longer. Give me back my wife, my family. I will take no man's hand until I have broken to pieces that creature HEEP! – In one week's time – at the hotel in Canterbury – I will tell all. – Go now."

I have never seen a man so excited. He ran out of the house.

But presently, a letter was brought, written at an inn nearby.

Sir,

I ask to be pardoned for my excitement. I hope that I made plain the fact that I shall meet you at the Ship Inn in Canterbury in one week's time.

Wilkins Micawber

In a week's time my aunt, Mr Dick and I went to Canterbury and found a note waiting for us in the inn telling us to expect Mr Micawber at half-past nine the next morning in the office of Wickfield and Heep.

We found Mr Micawber at his desk, writing.

"How do you do, Mr Micawber?" I said.

"Mr Copperfield," said Mr Micawber gravely, "I hope I see you well. Mr Wickfield is ill in bed, but Miss Wickfield will be happy to see her old friends."

He opened the door of the sitting room and said: "Miss Trotwood, Mr David Copperfield and Mr Dick."

I could see that our visit surprised Uriah Heep, who was in the room alone, but a moment later he was as humble as ever.

"Well," he said, "this is an unexpected pleasure. Things are changed in this office, Miss Trotwood, since I was a humble clerk."

Agnes came in. She seemed anxious and tired. Uriah watched her while she greeted us.

"Don't wait, Micawber," said Uriah. – "What are you waiting for? Micawber! Did you hear me tell you not to wait?"

"Yes," said Mr Micawber, without moving.

"Then why do you wait?"

"Because I wish to!" said Mr Micawber.

Uriah's cheeks became white.

"If there is a scoundrel upon earth, that scoundrel's name is HEEP!"

Uriah fell back as if he had been struck.

"Oh! This has been planned. You have arranged to meet here. You have been giving my clerk money to set him against me, Copperfield! Now, take care. You'll make nothing of this. I know your tricks. Micawber, go! I'll talk to you later."

My friend Traddles came in, leading Mrs Heep.

"Who are you?" said Uriah.

"I am a friend of Mr Wickfield," said Traddles, "and I have power to act for him."

"Uriah," said Mrs Heep.

"Be silent!" cried Uriah. – I always knew that his pretence at being humble was unreal!

Mr Micawber stood up and took out a large piece of paper. He began to read:

> *The business of Wickfield and Heep was done by Heep alone. Heep did everything. And Heep is a thief.*

Uriah ran forward and tried to seize the letter, but Mr Micawber struck his hand so that it fell, as if broken.

"If you come near me again, I'll break your head," said Micawber. He went on reading.

> *I was paid one pound a week. The rest was made to depend on the value of my work – and that meant on the baseness of my name, on the wrong I was able to do for Heep. He lent me money, and this put me still further in his power. I found that my services were needed to help him in deceiving Mr Wickfield.*

Mr Micawber looked round to see the effect of his words. Then he continued:

> *Mr Wickfield was deceived in every way, while Heep was saying all the time how grateful he was to him, how much he was his friend. – At last my heart was changed, changed by the thought of Miss Wickfield. I began to look into things secretly. He persuaded Mr Wickfield to sign important papers, saying that they were unimportant. He persuaded Mr Wickfield to allow him to draw out from the bank £1,200 belonging to Miss Trotwood saying that it was for certain things which had already been paid for. He made this seem as if Mr*

Wickfield had done it, and he has used it ever since as a way of forcing Mr Wickfield to do anything he wanted. I lived in Heep's house after he left it. I found the remains of a pocket-book which he had burnt.

"Uriah! Uriah!" cried Mrs Heep, "be humble. Make some arrangement with them."

I know that on many occasions Heep has changed the account books. He also made Mr Wickfield sign a paper showing that money had been lent to Mr Wickfield to save him from dishonour, although this money had never been lent. I have also a paper on which he practised signing Mr Wickfield's name.

Heep took his keys and began to open a certain cupboard. Clearly he meant to look in it for the papers Mr Micawber had mentioned. But suddenly he thought of what he was doing and turned again towards us.

"Uriah," said his mother, "be humble and make an arrangement. When Mr Traddles told me upstairs that he had found out everything, I promised him that you would be humble and pay back the money."

Mr Micawber went on:

I can show that Heep forced Mr Wickfield to take him as a partner, promising to pay him a certain amount of money every year; that he pretended to lend money to Mr Wickfield (this money being Mr Wickfield's own money), and so got him into his power.
I shall prove these things are true, and then I shall, with my unhappy family, disappear from the world in which we have been so unworthy.

Mr Micawber finished his reading. He handed the paper

to my aunt.

Uriah went to the cupboard again and opened it. It was empty.

"Where are the account books?" he cried. "Some thief has taken the books."

"I did," said Mr Micawber.

"I have them," said Traddles.

My aunt suddenly ran at Uriah and seized him.

"Do you know what I want?" she said. "I want my money. Agnes, my dear, so long as I believed that Mr Wickfield had taken my money I would not say a word! But now I know that this fellow did it, and I'll have it."

Uriah sat down.

"What do you want me to do?" he said.

"You will sign a paper," said Traddles, "giving everything to me. If you don't, you will go to prison."

Mrs Heep broke out again, begging Agnes to help them and to have mercy.

"Mother!" Uriah said. "Stop that noise! Well, let me have the paper. I'll sign it."

We were all very grateful to Mr Micawber and eager to tell him so. We went home with him. His house was not far off. The street door opened into the sitting room, and he ran in.

"Emma!" he cried, and rushed into Mrs Micawber's arms.

"Emma," he said, "the cloud has passed from my mind. Now welcome hunger and rags! Our trust in each other will support us to the end."

"Mr Micawber," said my aunt, "I wonder that you have never thought of going out of England – to some other land, to Australia, perhaps."

"I have long dreamt of doing so," said Mr Micawber (though I believe he had never thought of it before). "But there is a difficulty."

"Money?" said my aunt. "But you are doing us a great service. We would like to give you the money."

"I could not receive it as a gift. But, if it could be lent to me . . ."

"Of course," said my aunt.

"Is the country of such a kind," asked Mrs Micawber, "that a man of Mr Micawber's powers would have a fair chance of rising? I would not expect him to become Governor, but might he find reasonable openings for his powers?"

"There is no better chance anywhere," said my aunt.

We walked through the market-place, and Mr Micawber had already begun to behave like an Australian farmer and looked at the sheep in a knowing way.

My aunt, Agnes and I went back to Canterbury to meet Traddles and deal with the business of Wickfield and Heep.

"Mr Wickfield is much better," said Traddles, when we had all met together. "He has been able to help us a great deal in getting things clear. Having got everything into order, I find that Mr Wickfield owes nothing to anyone. There is a small amount – some hundreds of pounds – on which he can live."

"Next, Miss Trotwood," continued Traddles. "Your money . . ."

"Well," said my aunt, "if it is gone, I can bear it. If it is not, I shall be glad to get it back."

"I can find only five . . ."

"Five thousand?" said my aunt. "Or five pounds?"

"Five thousand," said Traddles.

"It was all there was," answered my aunt. "When I lost the money, I thought that Mr Wickfield had used it. Deceived by Heep, he wrote me a mad letter, saying that he was a thief. I visited him early one morning. I burnt his letter and told him that, if he could set things right, he should do so, and, if he could not, he should keep silent."

"What happened to Heep?" said my aunt.

"I don't know. He left here."

"And now, about Mr Micawber," said my aunt.

"Well, really," said Traddles, "I must give Mr Micawber high praise. He might have been paid highly by Uriah Heep to keep silent. – He owes one hundred and three pounds."

"Agnes, my dear, what shall we give him? Five hundred pounds?"

"I think it would be better," said Traddles, "to pay for his journey to Australia and give him a small amount of money for his use there."

Mr and Mrs Micawber were called into the room. My aunt told him what we had arranged.

"Now my advice to you," I said, "is never to allow anyone to lend you money again."

"Never," said Mr Micawber. "I shall write that vow upon the white page of my future life. I hope that my son Wilkins will always remember that he had far better put his hand in the fire than let it touch those creatures, money lenders, who have poisoned the life-blood of his unhappy parent."

Chapter 12
The last chapter

Agnes, Traddles and I went down to Gravesend to see the Micawbers start for Australia.

The Micawber children were all crying. They held on to Agnes's hands to the last. Then they went off in a boat to the ship. Traddles told us that at the last moment Mr Micawber had been taken to prison for debt, but that he, Traddles, had paid the money and set him free.

All visitors were leaving the ship. The time was come. I said goodbye. We got down into our boat and waited to see the ship start. It was a calm and beautiful sunset.

There was silence for a moment. Then the sails rose to the wind, and the ship began to move.

I travelled in Italy and France and Switzerland. At last I returned home. I went to my aunt's house at Dover, and was received by her, Mr Dick and dear Peggotty (who now acted as housekeeper) with tears of joy.

My aunt and I talked far into the night.

"And when, Trot, are you going over to Canterbury?" said my aunt.

"I shall ride over tomorrow morning," I answered.

I sat looking thoughtfully into the fire. I was thoughtful because I felt sorry for what I had failed to learn in my younger life.

"You will find her father a white-haired old man," said my aunt. "You will find her as good, as beautiful, as unselfish as she has always been."

"Has Agnes any—"

"What? Any what?" said my aunt sharply.

"Any admirers?" I said.

"Twenty!" cried my aunt. "She might have married twenty times."

"But is there any admirer who is worthy of her? Does she love one?"

"I think there is one," said my aunt. "She has never told me – but I think so."

I rode away early in the morning. When I got to Canterbury, I asked the new servant who opened the door to tell Miss Wickfield that a gentleman wished to see her.

I heard a door open, and I turned round. Her beautiful calm eyes met mine as she came towards me. She stopped, and laid her hand upon her heart.

"Agnes, my dear girl, I have come too suddenly, without warning."

"No, no. I am so glad to see you, Trotwood."

We sat down, side by side. She was so true, so beautiful, so good. I tried to bless her, to thank her, to tell her what she had done for me.

"And now, Agnes," I said, "tell me about yourself."

"What should I tell?" she said. "Father is well. You see us here, quiet in our own home."

There was silence for a moment.

"You are thoughtful, Trotwood."

"Agnes, shall I tell you what I am thinking about? I have been told that there is someone you love. Do not shut me out of something that is so important to your happiness. If you can trust me ..."

She rose. She put her hands to her face, and broke into such tears as struck me to the heart.

"Agnes, sister, dearest! What have I done?"

Agnes

"Let me go away, Trotwood. I'm not well. I'll speak to you – another time."

I took her in my arms. "Agnes, always my guide and best support."

Close in my arms she lay, nearer to my heart, her hand upon my shoulder, her sweet eyes shining through her tears on mine.

"I went away, Agnes, loving you. I stayed away, loving you. I returned home, loving you."

She laid her gentle hands upon my shoulders and looked calmly in my face.

"There is one thing I must say," she whispered.

"Dearest, what? Tell me."

"I have loved you all my life."

Questions

Questions on each chapter

1
1 Why was Mrs Copperfield sad?
2 Who told Miss Trotwood that the baby was a boy?
3 Who came to the door with David's mother?
4 Where did Peggotty's brother live?

2
1 What was the Peggottys' house?
2 What was Mr Peggotty's work?
3 Who was David's "new father"?

3
1 What was the first name of David's mother?
2 What did Mr Murdstone threaten to do to David?
3 What did Miss Murdstone ask for? Why?
4 When did David enjoy his lessons?
5 What was David's "only happiness"?
6 What did David do to Mr Murdstone?
7 What did Mr Murdstone do to David?

4
1 How long did David stay locked in his room?
2 Who spoke to him through the keyhole?
3 What did Peggotty give David?
4 What was the message from the carrier to Peggotty?
5 Who ate most of David's dinner?
6 What was the name of the school?
7 Who was the headmaster?
8 Who became David's best friend?
9 Why did Mr Murdstone call David "sullen"?
10 David had to leave Salem House. What had happened?
11 Why did Mr Barkis and Peggotty go into the church?

5
1 Whose house did David live in?
2 What did other people want when they went to the house?
3 Why was Mr Micawber taken to prison?

4 How did David lose his money and his box?
5 How much did he get for his coat?

6 1 What was Mr Dick's first piece of advice?
2 What was Mr Dick's second piece of advice?
3 Why did Mr and Miss Murdstone come to the cottage?
4 What was David's new name?

7 1 Who was Mr Wickfield's "little housekeeper"?
2 Who was the headmaster of David's new school?
3 What was the "humble work" of Uriah's father?
4 How often did Mr Dick visit David in Canterbury?

8 1 Why was David unable to keep secrets from Uriah Heep and his mother?
2 Who wanted to be introduced to Uriah and his mother?
3 Why did David run towards the Micawbers' inn?
4 What change had David noticed in Mr Wickfield?

9 1 Why did David ask Uriah to his lodgings?
2 Why did Uriah want to get Mr Wickfield in his power?
3 Mr Barkis "went out with the tide". What does that mean?

10 1 Why had Miss Trotwood come to London?
2 Why was she sorry for David?
3 What work did Agnes suggest for David?
4 What had "turned up" for Mr Micawber?

11 1 Whose health did Uriah want to drink to?
2 Where did Mr Micawber want to meet David?
3 Who were in the room when Traddles came in?
4 What did Uriah pay Micawber to do?
5 Why did Uriah begin to open a cupboard?
6 Where were the account books from the cupboard?
7 Where did Miss Trotwood suggest Mr Micawber should go?
8 How much of Miss Trotwood's money was saved?

12 1 Mr Micawber had vowed never to borrow money again. How do we know whether he kept that vow?
2 What did David think his aunt meant by "I think there is one [she loves]"?
3 What did Agnes confess to David?

Questions on the whole story

These are harder questions. Read the Introduction, and think hard about the questions before you answer them. Some of them ask for your opinion, and there is no fixed answer.

1 It will help you if you make a map to show David Copperfield's movements in England. Suppose that he was born at Blundeston, sixteen kilometres south of (Great) Yarmouth. What other places will you show on the map?

2 David Copperfield's mother:
 a Can you explain, with examples, her relations with:
  1 David? 2 Peggotty? 3 Mr Murdstone?
  4 Miss Murdstone?
 b Why do you think she married Mr Murdstone?
 c How intelligent do you think she was?
 d Miss Trotwood said that Mr Murdstone hated David because the sight of David made him remember how cruel he was to David's mother (page 34). Do you think this was true?

3 Mr Murdstone and Miss Murdstone:
 a Which of them was the less pleasant character in your opinion? Can you give a reason for your answer?
 b How did they treat: 1 David? 2 Peggotty?

4 Betsy Trotwood:
 a In what ways is she a most unusual person?
 b What did she do when she was "ruined"?
 c How did she help: 1 David? 2 Agnes? 3 the Micawbers?

5 Uriah Heep:
 a How does Dickens make the reader dislike him from his first appearance in the story?
 b What happens to him in the end? Do you think this is the right ending for him?

6 What is your opinion of Agnes's character?

7 Why was Mr Wickfield so easily cheated by Uriah Heep?

8 The story is told in the first person ("I", "me", "my", etc).
 a Why did Charles Dickens do this?
 b What advantages are there?

New words

autobiography
a book telling the story of the writer's own life. Adj: **autobiographical**

carrier
a carter who carried things locally

coach
a carriage with two to four horses and seats for about twelve passengers

expenses
money one spends

income
all the money one receives

optimist
one who expects that the future will be good; this state of mind is **optimism**

outcast
a person who has been thrown out from the company of other people

partner
a person who shares a business

scoundrel
a thoroughly bad man

short
in short = in few words

slap
hit with the open hand

sullen
silently bad-tempered

turn up
happen by good luck